Oscar's
Lonely
Christmas

Oscar's
Lonely
Christmas

by Holly Webb

tiger tales

5 River Road, Suite 128, Wilton, CT 06897
Published in the United States 2019
Originally published in Great Britain 2010
as *Oscar's Lonely Christmas* by the Little Tiger Group
Text copyright © 2010 Holly Webb
Cover illustration copyright © 2010 Sophy Williams
Inside illustration copyright © 2010 Katherine Kirkland
ISBN-13: 978-1-68010-448-6
ISBN-10: 1-68010-448-9
Printed in China
STP/1800/0255/0219
10 9 8 7 6 5 4 3 2 1

For more insight and activities, visit us at www.tigertalesbooks.com

Contents

Chapter One
Exciting News

Hannah took off her gloves and stuffed them in her pockets. The cold wind was stinging her cheeks, and she looked up at the sky hopefully. Maybe it would snow soon. It was only November, but it was so cold already! She reached into the bucket of winter bird food and scooped out a big helping, scattering it over the bird table.

Then she smiled to herself. She was sure she could hear some sparrows in the winter jasmine that was growing up the fence. They were scuffling around eagerly, waiting for her to go so that they could swoop in on the delicious mealworms that were their favorite part of the mixture.

She closed the bucket and put on her gloves again—it was so cold that her fingers had already started to hurt. Then she crept quietly back to the garden bench and curled up in the corner. If she was very, very quiet and still, the birds might come while she was there. It would make more sense to go inside and watch from her bedroom window, but she loved seeing the birds up close. They were so funny, the way they squabbled and shoved each other off the bird feeders. Hannah's family had five different bird feeders, and their yard was very popular with the local birds.

Hannah watched, snuggled inside her big scarf and furry hat, smiling to herself as a robin bossily sent all the other birds flapping off into the bushes. She wasn't going to be able to stay out here much longer; she could hardly feel her fingers. Hugging herself, she slipped into her favorite daydream—that she was cuddled up with a dog next to her, keeping her warm. Almost any dog would do, to be honest. She would really love a big dog that she could hug, but even a little dog would be wonderful.

Of course, as this was a daydream, she might as well have her all-time favorite. Daydream-Hannah sat there with her arms around a huge, black-and-white spotted Dalmatian. Just like Pongo from her favorite movie, *101 Dalmatians*. Hannah had watched both versions over and over, and Dalmatians were her dream dogs.

Hannah's mom and dad had been thinking about getting a dog for a while—at least, they always *said*, "We'll think about it" whenever Hannah asked. Her dad was very much into the idea. He loved going on long walks, and he'd shown her pictures of the dog he'd had when he was a boy. But Hannah's mom was a little anxious about Zach, Hannah's younger brother. She was worried that a dog wasn't a good idea with a toddler around. But Zach was almost three, and Hannah had started dropping hints about dogs again. She didn't think a dog would be a problem for Zach at all—he loved animals as much as Hannah did, and whenever he met a dog, he always wanted to hug it. It was more likely that the dog would need protection from Zach than the other way around.

Just as she was thinking about her little brother, Hannah heard the kitchen door bang, and he stumbled out into the yard, calling her name.

Hannah gave an annoyed little sigh as Zach frightened all the birds away. She'd been enjoying the peaceful moment without him around.

But as he wobbled around the corner of the house, she couldn't help smiling. Zach was wearing his big red snowsuit, and it was so stiff and padded that he could hardly move. He looked as though someone had inflated him like a balloon.

"Hannah! Hannah!" He came over and grabbed her hand. "Mommy wants you!"

Hannah's mom was coming out now, too, a big scarf wrapped around her neck. "You must be frozen sitting out here for so long! Did you see any interesting birds?"

Hannah shook her head. "Only the usual ones. I was about to come in since it's getting dark."

Mom was beaming. "We came out to tell you some news! I've just had a phone call—one I wasn't expecting." She took a deep breath. "It was from the lady who runs Dashing Dalmatians."

Hannah sat bolt upright, staring wide-eyed at her mom. "Is that—is that a Dalmatian *rescue*?" she asked. "Why did she call you?"

Her mom smiled even more widely. "Because I called her a few weeks ago to ask if she could keep an eye out for a young Dalmatian for us."

Hannah sprang off the bench and threw her arms around her mom. "Really? You didn't tell me! We're going to get a Dalmatian puppy? You mean it?"

Mom nodded. "Let's go and talk about this inside. I'm freezing!"

Hannah raced into the house, tugging off her coat and scarf, and unzipping Zach from his suit. She ran to put her things away, then skidded back into the kitchen. "Please tell me!"

Her mom laughed. "I should agree

to getting a puppy more often…. Yes, your dad and I decided that maybe you and Zach were old enough now for us to have a dog. Your dad wanted a big dog and you were desperate for a Dalmatian, so we found this lady— Lisa is her name—on the internet. She lives about 20 miles away, close to Lake Mills."

Hannah nodded. Lake Mills was a little town she'd visited on a school trip to see the working watermill.

"She runs a Dalmatian rescue—they don't get very many dogs given up to them, so we thought we'd have to wait a while. But they've just been asked to find a home for an adorable puppy." Her mom frowned. "She said something about him being given up because he didn't have the right markings. Lisa said she'd explain it all when we went to see the puppy, but he's really handsome, and very friendly."

"When can we go and see the puppy?" Hannah gasped. She hardly knew what to say—she felt so excited.

"How about tomorrow? Oooh, Hannah, don't squash me!" Her mom laughed as Hannah flung her arms around her waist. "So, you're happy, then? You haven't changed your mind about Dalmatians?"

"Of course not!" Hannah cried. "They're the

16

best dogs ever! We're really going to see some tomorrow?"

"Absolutely. It had to be a Saturday so your dad can come, too." Mom smiled. "He's going to get a big surprise when he gets home!"

Hannah's dad was just as excited as she was about the puppy. Mom told him all about the phone call over dinner.

"That's just such good news," he said. "I thought we'd have to wait a long time. We wanted to make sure we got a puppy from someone who really knows about Dalmatians. They can be a little nervous and excitable, and you have to be careful. Mom said the lady from Dashing Dalmatians was very nice when she called her. She gave her all sorts of test results and told her a lot about the breed." Then he frowned and glanced over at Hannah's mom. "I just thought of something. We did say we were going to try to avoid getting a puppy around Christmas, though, didn't we?"

Hannah's mom nodded slowly. "Oh, goodness, I'd forgotten about that. I just didn't think." She paused for a moment. "Lisa said we could take our puppy home next week. So that would be the first week of December. Oh, that *is* a little close to Christmas."

"Why can't we get the puppy before Christmas?" Hannah asked, her voice starting to squeak with panic—they couldn't change their minds now!

Her dad rubbed her shoulder. "It's just that Mom and I said that we wouldn't ever get a dog as a Christmas present— so many puppies end up at rescues after Christmas. And it's a stressful time for a dog, with so many people around, and the house all turned upside down."

"But you aren't getting us a dog for Christmas!" Hannah pointed out quickly, her heart thudding with hope. "The puppy just happens to be coming close to Christmas, that's all. It doesn't really make the puppy a Christmas present!" She dug her fingers into her hands, looking anxiously from Mom to Dad. Then she added, in case that had sounded greedy, "But I don't want anything else for Christmas; it's okay.

Just maybe a dog leash?"

Dad laughed. "Don't worry. I'm not saying we can't get a puppy. I was just wondering if now was the best time. But to be honest, I'm sure getting a puppy is a big upheaval whenever you do it."

"So … can we still go tomorrow?" Hannah whispered.

Her mom and dad exchanged a look and smiled.

"Yes," Mom told her. "We'll go."

"Please-may-I-leave-the-table?" Hannah rattled off. "I don't want any dessert, thanks. I'm going to go and look up Dalmatians on the computer!"

Chapter Two
Meeting the Puppies

Hannah sat in the back of the car next to Zach, biting her lip. Mom had gotten sick of her asking if they were almost there, and she'd told Hannah she'd turn the car around if she said it again. It was just that she was desperate to know!

"Look, there's a sign for Lake Mills," Dad said, taking pity on her. "Not far now."

Hannah nodded, staring hopefully out the window. Then she laughed and pointed at a sign in the front yard of a house just ahead. "Look! It's all spotted!"

Mom put her turn signal on. "That has to be it," she said. "Yes, it says Dashing Dalmatians." She parked the car in the driveway.

Hannah could hear excited barking as she got out of the car, and ran around to help Zach unbuckle his car seat harness. "We're here, Zach! Going to see the dogs!"

"Dogs!" Zach clapped his hands excitedly.

A friendly-looking woman was opening the door of the house, and beside her—Hannah caught her breath at the sight—were two big Dalmatians. They were so beautiful, snow-white, with a dappling of glossy black spots all over.

"Dog! Dog!" Zach squeaked delightedly, jumping up and down and pulling on Hannah's hand.

The owner of the dogs laughed. "Somebody's excited! I'm Lisa. And these are Tucker and Trixie. They're very friendly; you can pet them. Just watch your little brother, though, okay? The dogs are a lot bigger than he is, and they might knock him over by accident."

Hannah nodded. "I'll hold his hand," she promised. "He loves dogs. We both do." She stretched out her free hand to

Trixie, who sniffed it interestedly and then gave her a gentle lick.

"Ugh!" Zach giggled.

"I don't mind," Hannah sighed and petted Trixie's soft nose and around her silky spotted ears. Trixie was so beautiful. And a dog just like Trixie might be theirs soon. It was hard to believe.

"Come inside and let me take your coats. We have a few puppies that are the perfect age to be adopted now," Lisa explained as she led Hannah's family through the house, with the two Dalmatians nosing at them inquisitively. "The one puppy that I told you about on the phone is seven weeks old. His spots have come through. Although he'll still get more, you can see what he's going to be like when he's older. And he's starting to really enjoy meeting people."

Hannah looked up at her mom and dad eagerly, and her dad squeezed her shoulder. "You look like you're about to meet the president!" he told her in a whisper.

"I feel like I am!" Hannah whispered back.

"This used to be a spare bedroom, before we started rescuing dogs!" Lisa explained as they came to a door at the end of the hallway. "Now we use it as a puppy room." She opened the door and led them in. A wire pen occupied about half the room—and Hannah saw five puppies, all different sizes. They were tumbling and squirming over each other in a black-and-white spotted mass.

"Oh, look at them!" Hannah breathed. "They're adorable!"

"We have five puppies with us right now," Lisa said. "It's the most we've ever had at one time. Four of them were found in an abandoned shed. An older couple happened to be out for a walk and heard the puppies whining, and they brought them to us."

Hannah leaned over the wire netting to see the puppies, and Zach followed her, cooing delightedly at the beautiful little animals. Tucker and Trixie watched Hannah and Zach closely, then looked up at Lisa as if to ask if the children were safe.

"It's all right," Lisa said gently.

"I can't tell them apart," Hannah said, sitting down to get a closer look at the puppies rolling around the pen. "Oh! Except that one! He has a patch around his tail! And I think he's a little bigger."

The patched puppy seemed to know he was being talked about. He padded over to the wire and looked at Hannah and Zach with his head to one side.

Hannah giggled at his funny little face, and the puppy jumped back in surprise.

"I'm sorry, I didn't mean to scare you," Hannah told him gently. "I only laughed because you're so sweet."

The puppy edged closer again and put out a bright pink tongue to lick Hannah's fingers—she'd been holding on to the wire without even realizing it.

"Me! Me!" Zach squeaked, making the puppy jump again. He eyed Zach suspiciously and took a step sideways, closer to Hannah. Then he leaned his head against the wire and looked up at her.

Hannah tried not to laugh and scare him again, but it was so difficult. It was almost as if the puppy was talking to her—*Scratch my ears, please.*

The puppy sighed delightedly as Hannah scratched behind his soft, white-dappled ears. This was good. The little one was loud and bouncy, but this girl was doing excellent ear-scratching. He glared at one of the other puppies as she came too close. The girl was his, and he had no intention of sharing. The other puppy trotted away, back to curl up with her brothers and sisters.

"Well, he's certainly taken to you," Lisa commented. She sounded happy, and Hannah glanced up at her hopefully. Did that mean they would be allowed to have a puppy? Maybe even—this puppy? Hannah could see that they were all beautiful, but this one just seemed to have chosen her.

Dad had crouched down next to

Hannah to look at the puppies. "Is there a particular puppy we can have?" he asked Lisa. "You mentioned something on the phone yesterday...."

Lisa nodded. "The four abandoned puppies were very small when they were brought in. We needed to give them all of their vaccinations and be sure that they were strong enough before we could let them be adopted. But they'll all be going to their new homes over the next few weeks."

Hannah's heart seemed to fall into her stomach. So she couldn't have one of these wonderful puppies? She looked down at her puppy, his eyes blissfully closed as she tickled him. He was so perfect....

"But there's a puppy that has just

come in—his owner really wanted a show dog, you see, and the puppy she brought in just won't be up to showing."

Mom looked confused. "Why not? They're all so beautiful. Can you really tell now whether they won't be show dogs?"

Hannah looked around, her eyes shining. "It's this puppy, isn't it? Please say it's this one!"

The puppy stared up at Lisa, too, as though he wanted to hear the news. He wagged his little whip-like tail with the pretty patch around the base.

"Yes." Lisa smiled at her. "How did you know?"

Hannah looked shy. She'd read so much about Dalmatians, but she was sure that Lisa knew a lot more, and she didn't want to sound silly. "They aren't really supposed to have patches, are they?" she asked. Lisa nodded encouragingly, so she went on. "The puppies are supposed to be born snow-white, and then the spots grow in when they're a couple of weeks old and they keep on growing for a while—until they're about a year old." She looked over at all the puppies. They were still mostly white, and their spots were only the size of raisins. "But sometimes you get puppies born with black patches." She rubbed the puppy's ears again. "But I've never seen a picture of a puppy with a patch on his tail!"

"Neither have I!" Lisa laughed. "He's really special. But he'd be no good in the show ring—they don't allow patches. So he can only ever be a pet."

She reached over the wire netting and gently picked up the puppy, and then she held him close to Hannah. "Would you like him on your lap?"

Hannah nodded. She held out her arms to cuddle the puppy, and he snuggled onto her lap. Zach sat next to her, patting the puppy on the bottom.

But Dad was looking worried. "If there's something wrong with him, maybe we should wait...."

"There's nothing wrong with him!" Hannah protested. Her voice was sharp with fear that Dad might say no, and the puppy's eyes widened. He whimpered, unsure what was wrong.

"Try not to speak too loudly," Lisa said, her voice soothing. "Dalmatians are very high-strung; you need to be calm and gentle."

"I'm sorry," Hannah whispered, half to Lisa and half to the puppy.

"You're doing really well," Lisa said reassuringly. Then she looked over at Hannah's dad. "He's perfectly healthy. You weren't planning to take him to shows, right?"

Hannah looked hopefully at her dad. "We just want him for a pet. And he might even be better than a regular Dalmatian," she whispered. "Sometimes they can be deaf, but the ones with patches usually hear fine."

Lisa laughed in surprise. "You really have been doing your homework."

"I love Dalmatians," Hannah told her. "I've been dreaming of having one ever since I can remember."

"Hannah's right about the deafness," Lisa explained to Hannah's mom and dad. "But he seems completely fine, and he's going to be tested next week."

"I know they need a lot of exercise, too, and they need to be around people. But Dad's going to take me and the puppy on long walks every day," Hannah explained. "And Mom and Zach are at home, even when I'm at school."

"That's great! Dalmatians have tons of energy, and they get bored very easily because they're so clever. You'll need to take him to training classes. I can recommend a good trainer close to you."

"So we can have him?" Hannah asked, cuddling the puppy close, and looking anxiously between Lisa and her mom and dad.

Lisa smiled. "I think you'd give him a wonderful home. He's really settled with you."

Dad nodded slowly, and Hannah laid her cheek gently against the puppy's soft head. He made a happy little cooing growl, and she giggled. "You're happy, too, aren't you, little pup?"

The puppy yawned hugely, showing his little pointy teeth, and curled up in Hannah's lap. He looked as though he wasn't going anywhere.

Mom reached down to pet him. "I don't think it's up to us at all. He's definitely chosen you, Hannah!"

Chapter Three
Oscar Comes Home

"We're bringing the puppy home next weekend!" Hannah whispered to her best friend, Nicky, at school on Monday.

"You're so lucky! I wish we could have a dog, but my mom just says we don't have time to take care of one."

"You can come on walks with us," Hannah offered.

"Oh, I think it's almost our turn!"

Nicky looked over at their teacher, Mr. Bradford, who was standing behind them at the back of the auditorium. "There's only Izzie and Ben before us."

Their class was auditioning for the school Christmas play. Hannah was hoping for a big part this year. She loved being in plays, but she always felt really nervous when they had to try out, and she'd never been given much to say before. She and Nicky had to read a scene from the play from up on the stage so Mr. Bradford could hear how loudly and clearly they could speak.

"Are you nervous?" Nicky whispered. "I am!"

Hannah smiled. Nicky was a wonderful dancer and had taken a lot of ballet classes. She was bound to be given a part with some dancing. "You know, I'm so excited about our puppy, I actually don't feel nervous at all!" she said. Usually nerves made her tummy feel funny.

"Okay, Nicky and Hannah!" Mr. Bradford called, looking at his list.

"Break a leg!" Hannah told Nicky, and they both crossed their fingers for luck.

Two days later, Hannah dashed out of school to tell her mom the good news.

Mom was waiting in the playground with Zach in his stroller. "Did you get a good part?" she asked, seeing Hannah's beaming face. The girls had

had to wait for Mr. Bradford to make up his mind. It was lucky that Hannah had been so excited about the puppy, or it would have been torture.

"I'm going to be the angel!" Hannah told Mom. "It's the main part, and I do all the storytelling! And Nicky's the innkeeper's daughter. She gets to dance."

"Congratulations, Hannah!" Her mom gave her a hug. "You'll have to tell Grandma when she comes over for dinner tonight."

"Dog?" Zach asked, seeing that everyone was happy and hoping it meant more puppies.

"Oh, sweetie, not yet. Soon," Mom promised as they headed out the gate. Zach was just as desperate as

Hannah for their puppy to come home, and he'd even taken to curling up on the soft blue dog cushion they had bought. They'd had to do a huge shopping trip at the pet store to get everything the puppy would need.

"Only a few more days!" Hannah beamed. "And the puppy is bringing me luck already. Maybe I'm going to be an Oscar-winning actress!" She stopped suddenly in the middle of the pavement. "Oscar! Mom, can we call the puppy Oscar? It's such a cute name."

Mom looked at her thoughtfully. "Hmm. I like it. Definitely better than Freckles and all those other spotty names we were thinking of."

"He looks like an Oscar," Hannah

said. Oscar. Her puppy. It was only a little while longer until he came home!

Hannah carried the puppy carefully into the kitchen. "Look, this is your bed." She gently set Oscar down next to the big blue cushion. The puppy looked at it thoughtfully. It was huge, but it looked comfy. He hopped his front paws up onto the edge of the cushion, and then scrambled to get his back paws on, too. He sniffed around the cushion, interested in the smell of newness. Then he looked hopefully at Hannah. The cushion was too big for him all by himself. Would she come and snuggle up with him?

"Dog bed!" Zach squawked, pushing

past Hannah and flinging himself onto the cushion with Oscar.

Oscar cowered back, horrified by this noisy thing that had almost landed on him. Whimpering, he wriggled off the cushion and slunk over to Hannah.

"I want do-og!" wailed Zach, and Mom picked him up.

Hannah gently scooped the puppy into her arms. "He really frightened Oscar!" she whispered angrily to Mom. She was trying hard not to sound too upset, after what Lisa had told them about Dalmatians being nervous.

"Zach doesn't really understand about being gentle," Dad explained. "He'll get there."

Hannah sniffed. Mom and Dad never scolded Zach—whenever he was naughty, they always said he was just little. Well, Oscar was littler! Hannah just hoped that Mom wouldn't let Zach upset Oscar while she was at school.

The first day with Oscar was so special. Hannah hardly left the kitchen. Oscar was going to stay in there for the first few days—with trips out into the yard to go to the bathroom, of course. She had bought him a special squeaky bone with her own money, and he loved it. He kept jumping on it and shaking it in his teeth, and then the bone would squeak, and he would look really surprised and drop it on the floor. Then he'd start all over again until he wore himself out. Hannah spent a long time curled up next to his cushion just watching him sleep. He was the most beautiful thing she had ever seen.

Oscar didn't spend that much of

his sleep time actually *on* his cushion. As soon as he'd finished exploring, he would wander back to wherever Hannah was and collapse on her— he particularly liked her feet, draping himself over them like a spotted, saggy little beanbag and falling fast asleep.

Hannah was worried that the first night was going to be really difficult. How could they leave Oscar all on his own downstairs? But Mom had been really firm from the beginning that Oscar was not allowed in her room. Mom said he would soon be much too big to sleep on her bed, even though he was tiny now. And there were a lot of things upstairs that she didn't want chewed.

Lisa had told them about a special

technique to get Oscar used to being left alone in the kitchen, and Hannah practiced it with him that afternoon. Mom took Zach out for a walk to get him out of the way, and Dad and Hannah padded around in the kitchen, with Oscar watching them. Then they went out, shutting the door.

"Can we go back in yet?" Hannah asked. "Dad, come on, Lisa said to go back before he gets upset! Remember, you're going to read the paper and pretend you aren't watching him."

Dad nodded and opened the kitchen door. Hannah glanced over at Oscar. He was looking puzzled and a little worried. She looked away again and went to put away some cups from the drying rack. Then she nudged Dad.

"Time to go again!"

They kept popping in and out, making sure that they always got back before Oscar cried. Eventually, he got bored watching and went to sleep.

"Lisa was right," Hannah whispered. "I hope it works tonight."

At bedtime, she took Oscar out for one last bathroom trip in the yard and made sure there was some newspaper down in the corner of the kitchen for the night. Then she closed the door behind her and looked hopefully at Mom and Dad.

"Lisa said he'd be sure that we're just on the other side of the door," Hannah said. "And he must be worn out from all the playing we've done." But as she pressed her ear to the door, she couldn't help feeling a little doubtful. There was no whining. Just a little tappity-tap of claws on tiles and a snuffling noise. Hannah held her breath.

On the other side of the door, Oscar sniffed thoughtfully, wondering if Hannah would come back in soon. Maybe with some more of those good meaty biscuits! He yawned and padded back to his cushion. He clambered up and flopped on top of his toy bone. It squeaked, and he gave it a half-hearted chew. Maybe if he went to sleep, it would be time to eat when he woke up....

Oscar curled up and closed his eyes— and out in the hall, Hannah grinned at her mom and dad. There was a little growly snore coming from behind the kitchen door. It had worked!

Chapter Four
The Trouble with Zach

Oscar soon settled into Hannah's house. He loved Hannah, and they spent hours playing, Oscar scampering around as she rolled his ball or threw his squeaky bone. After the first couple of days, once Oscar was allowed out of the kitchen, Hannah discovered that he loved to curl up on the couch with her while she read or watched TV.

Mom wasn't sure about this at first. "When he gets to his full size, he'll take up half the couch just by himself," she complained. But she gave in eventually when Oscar sat on her feet while she was watching her favorite TV show after she'd put Zach to bed. He sat there staring up at her lovingly, and Mom couldn't resist. She sighed and patted the couch, and Oscar scrambled and wriggled his way up. Then he lay there next to Mom with his head in her lap, slowly thumping his tail on the cushions.

Oscar's only problem was Zach. It wasn't that Zach didn't like him—the little boy adored him and wanted to be with him all the time. He just wouldn't leave the puppy alone. Zach wanted to cuddle Oscar on his cushion. He wanted to snuggle up with him on the couch. He even wanted to eat his food out of a bowl like Oscar's.

A week after Oscar came home with them, Hannah was up in her room learning her lines for the play when she heard a strange noise on the stairs. A whimpering noise, mixed with bumps, and panting. That was Oscar whimpering—and it sounded like Zach was with him! She flung down her script and dashed out of her bedroom. As she'd suspected, Zach was halfway up the stairs, with Oscar dangling from his arms, looking panicked.

"Want Ossa in my bed!" Zach wailed when he saw Hannah coming down the stairs looking angry.

"You know we aren't allowed!" Hannah told him furiously. Why did Zach always think he could get away with everything? It wasn't as if she wouldn't like Oscar in *her* bed! Oscar wriggled and whimpered again, and Hannah stretched out her arms to him.

But Zach wouldn't let go. "My dog!" he whined.

"Zach! You're making him sad. Stop it! Give him to me!" Hannah was trying not to shout and upset Oscar, but it was hard when she really wanted to yell at Zach.

"Don't want to!"

"Now!" Hannah hissed.

"No!" Zach burst into tears as Oscar finally wriggled out of his grip and scrambled into Hannah's arms.

"Hannah! What are you doing with Oscar—you know he's not allowed upstairs!" Mom had come out into the hallway, and she was glaring at Hannah.

"But I wasn't…!" Hannah gasped.

"And what did you do to upset Zach?" Mom gave her an accusing look as she picked Zach up. He was really howling.

Hannah shook her head in amazement. It was so unfair. Sometimes she didn't know how Zach managed it. He *never* got into trouble.

After she'd caught Zach taking Oscar upstairs, Hannah made a real effort to keep an eye on her little brother and make sure he wasn't bothering Oscar too much. She was glad when he had had all his vaccinations, and she and Dad could take him out for long walks. Oscar loved it, especially when they took him to the woods. He even loved splashing in the stream, despite the December cold.

One Sunday, Hannah finally persuaded Mom and Dad to let her and Nicky take Oscar for a walk on their own, now that Oscar was used to being on the leash. They agreed the girls could go as long as they borrowed Hannah's mom's cell phone and promised to be back in half an hour.

"We don't really have time to go all the way to the woods. Should we go to the park?" Nicky suggested.

Hannah looked thoughtful. "Oh, I know! Let's go and show Oscar the horses in the field down past school! Dalmatians used to be carriage dogs who ran alongside coaches hundreds of years ago. They're supposed to love horses, and I don't think Oscar's ever seen any. Should I head back and tell Mom that's where we're going?"

Nicky nodded eagerly and smiled with pride when Hannah passed her Oscar's leash.

Oscar gazed up at the new girl with interest. She wasn't like Hannah, but she was nice. He then looked hopefully toward the house, waiting for Hannah to come back. When she came running down the path, he yapped happily and danced around her feet.

"He really loves you," Nicky sighed. "You're so lucky!"

"I know." Hannah nodded. "I love you, too, Oscar," she told him, rubbing his ears.

Nicky looked back at the house. "Oh, Zach's waving to us. He looks a little sad; I bet he wishes he could come, too."

Hannah groaned. "He's being such

a nightmare at the moment! He won't leave Oscar alone, and Mom keeps making excuses for him. Yesterday he decided he wanted to feed Oscar, and he poured a whole bag of the special dog treats into his bowl, so of course Oscar ate them!" She sighed. "And you know what Mom said? That I should have made sure I put the treats away in the cupboard."

Nicky giggled. "Sometimes I'm glad I'm the youngest!"

The horses the girls were going to see belonged to a riding school, and there were usually a few of them out in one of the fields. At the moment, they were wrapped up in rugs and not out for the whole day, but Hannah was pretty sure there would be something for Oscar to see.

Oscar trotted along happily, enjoying the interesting smells and listening to the girls chatting.

"Oh, look, they *are* out!" Hannah said, quickening her pace. "Come on, Oscar." They hurried up to the field to look at the horses, and Hannah picked Oscar up, resting his front paws on the top of the fence. She could feel his tail wagging against her arms, and it made her giggle.

Oscar gazed across the field at the horses, enchanted by the huge creatures. He'd seen other dogs, but never anything as tall and graceful as these.

At last Hannah sighed. "We should get back, or Mom will be worried. I promise I'll bring you to see them again, Oscar."

Hannah wished she could take Oscar out for a long walk every day, but now that it was getting closer to Christmas, the school play was taking up a lot more of her time. Mr. Bradford insisted that everyone had to know their lines perfectly, and he'd planned some extra rehearsals for the main parts after school. Hannah had to go to all of them because her big role meant that she was in every scene.

Hannah loved being in the play, and so far, she was dealing with her nerves really well. But the extra rehearsals made it hard to fit in Oscar's walks. By the time she got home from school, it was totally dark—and there was no way Mom would let her walk Oscar in the woods. They had to make do with a quick jog around the park with Dad when he got home. Other than that, it was up to Mom to take Oscar for a walk in the morning. But that meant Mom had to have Oscar and Zach's stroller, which wasn't very easy. Hannah had been hoping they could start dog-training classes soon, too, but Mom said that with all the rehearsals, there was no way Hannah could fit in anything else. They would have to wait until after Christmas.

Oscar really missed his walks. It seemed like forever since he'd had a good one, and Hannah hardly seemed to be at home at all. He was sick of watching the door, waiting for Hannah to come home. Why wasn't she back?

He thoughtfully sniffed the shoe rack in the hallway and tugged at a trailing pink shoelace. One of Mom's sneakers fell down, and he nudged it with his nose. This was fun! He growled at it, pretending it was something to chase, and then held it down with his front paws and started to gnaw at the laces.

Just then, Mom came down the stairs. "Oscar, no! No chewing! Bad dog!" She snatched the sneaker back and shooed him into the kitchen.

Oscar slumped down on his cushion

and licked his nose sadly. He didn't really understand what he'd done wrong. He wanted to go out and have a nice long run with Hannah. She was still Oscar's favorite person, but she was never there. Why didn't she want to spend time with him anymore? He felt bored and grumpy, and that made him want to chew things. He didn't know he wasn't allowed to chew shoes....

He was still looking miserable when Hannah got home at last. She sat down by his cushion to pet him. "Mom told me about her shoe. I'm sorry she was upset with you, Oscar. You were just bored, weren't you, poor baby." Hannah sighed. "It isn't long until the play now. After that, we'll go on a lot more walks, I promise."

Chapter Five
Disaster!

Oscar sat on the back of the couch and stared out the window, watching for Hannah in the gathering dark. He missed her. It seemed so long since she'd left the house for school that morning. She had taken him out in the yard and they'd played with his jingly ball, which had been fun. But then Hannah's mom had called her in. Since then he'd only had a quick walk around the park at lunchtime, with Zach trying to hold his leash, and pulling him backward and forward.

"Ossa!"

It was Zach again, running into the living room. Oscar whipped his head around and lost his balance. He slid down between the couch and the window, yelping with fright, although he wasn't really hurt, only surprised.

Zach clambered onto the couch and hung perilously over the back, looking for Oscar.

Oscar whimpered miserably. He wanted to be left alone until Hannah came back. He started to creep along behind the couch, meaning to dash out the living-room door. Hannah's mom was preparing dinner in the kitchen, so she could let him out into the yard, and then he'd be safely away from Zach bothering him and pulling at his ears.

But Zach could move surprisingly fast. He wriggled down from the back of the couch and trotted around to meet Oscar as he emerged from behind it.

"Ossa!" The little boy flung his arms around the puppy's neck, squeezing him lovingly.

Oscar moaned. Zach was cuddling him much too tightly, and it hurt. He tried to pull back out of Zach's arms, but that only made Zach hold him tighter. Oscar wriggled and struggled, and Zach giggled, thinking it was all just a funny game.

Oscar was starting to feel desperate.

He wanted to snap, but he knew he shouldn't. Instead, he growled. A low *Rrrrrrrrrrr!* deep in his chest, his lips drawing back from his teeth in a snarl.

Zach let go of Oscar, stumbling away, his eyes wide with fright.

Oscar shot out into the hallway, looking for a place to hide in case Zach followed him. There was a little alcove under the stairs where everyone kept their coats and bags, and Oscar scurried into it, hiding behind Hannah's ballet bag. His heart was racing, and he felt grumpy and scared at the same time. He hadn't wanted to upset the little boy, but why wouldn't Zach just leave him alone?

His ears pricked up as he heard Hannah coming up the front path, followed by her dad, who'd gone to pick her up from the rehearsal. He longed to leap out and run to her—but Zach might grab him again. Better to stay hidden. He crouched down behind the bag, still shivering.

"Oscar?" Hannah sounded surprised. Usually he was there, dancing around her as soon as she came in the door, but today he was nowhere to be seen.

"I wonder if he got shut in somewhere," Dad suggested as Hannah went to put her school bag away under the stairs.

As soon as he saw her, Oscar wriggled out on his tummy, making a little whining noise.

"Oh! He's here! Oscar, what's the matter? Dad, he's shaking." Hannah knelt down to cuddle him, and Oscar snuggled against her gratefully.

"Ossa growled," a small voice said behind Hannah, and she turned around to find Zach standing in the living-room doorway, looking half-guilty, half-scared.

Dad frowned. "What happened, Zach?" he asked.

Mom rushed out into the hall. "Oh, no! What's the matter? I was just putting the pasta on, and I couldn't hear anything over the sound of the kettle."

"Zach's been bothering Oscar again, I bet!" Hannah burst out. She had felt Oscar tense up as soon as Zach appeared.

"Don't always blame Zach, Hannah. He's only little," Mom said gently.

Hannah sighed.

"Zach, were you chasing Oscar?" Dad asked, looking into Zach's eyes.

Zach wriggled away from him. "No. Jus' petting."

"You have to be gentle, Zach," Dad explained. "He's only a puppy."

Hannah glared at Zach. He'd gotten away with it, again! It just wasn't fair! As she cuddled Oscar closer, she could feel how upset he was. She only wished she could have been there to protect him.

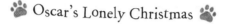

"I have to make some wings as part of my costume," Hannah told everyone at the dinner table later on. "Mr. Bradford is going to give me some tissue paper to bring home." She smiled to herself, but it wasn't because of her excitement about her beautiful angel costume. Under the table, a small, warm muzzle was resting lovingly on her foot. Hannah lifted a piece of meat on her fork and "accidentally" dropped it down the side of her chair. Oscar deserved a treat. A little black-and-white-blur raced to snap it up.

"What else are you wearing, do you know?" Mom asked.

"A gold tunic thing and a halo," Hannah told her. "Mrs. Garner is making the halo. She's the lady who comes in to help with art. She's

74

wonderful at making things."

"Sounds good." Dad smiled. "I'm really looking forward to seeing this show next week. We've heard so much about it, I feel like I could join in!"

Hannah grinned. She had gone on about the play a bit, she supposed.

She brought home all the pieces for the wings that Friday. They were very complicated to make, and Dad had to help her over the weekend. Hannah cut out all the tissue paper feathers, and Dad made her a wire frame to stick them on and helped her tie ribbons on to fasten the wings around her shoulders. They worked on them for two whole evenings, dabbing on gold paint here and there, and making them look really special.

So it was a total disaster when Hannah came home from school on Monday, the day before the dress rehearsal, and found her wings lying on the living-room floor with half the feathers ripped off.

"Mom!" Hannah called out, horrified. Mom rushed in from the hallway, where she'd been taking off Zach's coat.

"What is it?"

"Why weren't you watching him?" Hannah wailed. "How could you let him tear them up like that? Why did you do it, Zach!" she shouted angrily as she saw Zach peeking around the door.

"Oh, Hannah, I don't think this was Zach," Mom said, shaking her head. "And don't yell at him, please. It's mean."

Hannah blinked. "Who was it, then?"

"Oscar! Look, they're all chewed. I'm sorry; we shouldn't have left them to dry on that low shelf, but I just didn't think about it." She sighed. "We need to be more careful." She looked down at Oscar, who'd just emerged from behind the couch. "No, Oscar! Look at this mess!"

"It wasn't Oscar," Hannah said stubbornly, sweeping him up in her arms. But she could see the white tissue paper sticking out of the corner of his mouth, and she knew that Mom was right. Cuddling Oscar tightly, she marched out of the living room. There was no way she was saying she was sorry to Zach.

Dad had helped Hannah remake her wings in time for the dress rehearsal, but they weren't quite as good as they'd been before. Hannah wriggled her shoulders nervously, fussing with the ribbons that held the wings on. She couldn't believe it was the night of the performance at last.

"Can you see them?" Nicky asked as Hannah peeked around the side of the curtain.

Hannah shook her head. "No. Oh, but your mom and dad are over there!" She frowned as she stared around the hall again. "They're going to have to sit in the back," she said. "It's really filling up."

Mom had promised Hannah that she and Dad would be there in plenty of time—they were going to leave Zach with Grandma. *So where were they?*

Somebody giggled loudly behind Hannah, making her jump. Everyone was chatting excitedly backstage. They'd brought sandwiches to school for a quick snack, so they could fit in one last run-through before that night's performance. The nerves had been building ever since the bell rang for the end of school. Hannah glanced down at the little photo in her hand, a favorite one of Oscar that she'd glued onto a card to keep in her school bag. She was feeling a little jittery about her part, and looking at Oscar's handsome face made her feel better.

There was a little flurry at the hall

doors, and Hannah's eyes widened. There was Grandma! She seemed to be explaining something to Mrs. Garner, who was taking the tickets.

But Grandma was supposed to be babysitting Zach. Hannah wished she could go and ask Grandma what was going on. But she had her costume on already, and the play was due to start in a few minutes. Hannah rubbed Oscar's photo with one finger, her tummy twisting. Why hadn't Mom and Dad come?

Chapter Six
Home Alone

Oscar padded into the hallway and went to sniff at the front door. Then he sat down for a couple of minutes before trailing back into the kitchen for a drink from his water bowl.

Where was everyone? Hannah's mom had taken Zach out as usual and come back on her own to make a cup of tea. But then the phone had rung, startling

Oscar out of his nap. He'd gotten up from his cushion, feeling sure it was close to dinner time, and hoping that if he stood next to Hannah's mom and wagged his tail, she might feed him.

But she had crashed the phone down so fast it fell out of its holder—and she hadn't even bothered to pick it up again! And then she ran out of the kitchen so fast that she fell over Oscar. She didn't stop to say she was sorry, or pet him, or even scold for being in her way. She simply dashed out of the house, without even a coat, and drove off in the car.

She still hadn't come back. Hannah should have been home from school by now, Oscar was sure. And Zach? Surely he should be home now, too. It felt close to the time that their dad should be back from work as well. Oscar didn't like being left on his own for so long, and he was getting really hungry now. He padded up the hallway again, his tail hanging low, and then suddenly brightened as he heard footsteps.

Slow, frightened footsteps, not Hannah's usual happy run. He backed away from the door, feeling anxious.

The door opened and Grandma came in, followed by Hannah, her angel wings trailing from her hand.

Hannah looked upset, and even though she hugged him, she felt different. She was holding him so tightly, and he could feel her heart thudding a fast, anxious beat. Oscar nuzzled her worriedly, wondering what was wrong.

"Oh, Oscar, didn't Mom feed you?"
Hannah held him in front of her,
looking into his eyes. "Poor Oscar, you
must be starving. Come on." Hannah
went to get his special dog biscuits.

Oscar waited by his bowl gratefully,
but he didn't feel as hungry as he had

before. He knew that something was wrong, and he hated seeing Hannah so unhappy. It made him feel jittery and nervous, and somehow all wrong.

After he'd eaten, he went to sit on the couch between Hannah and Grandma. They had the television on, but they weren't really paying attention to it. It got later and later, and Oscar finally fell asleep on the couch, curled up against Hannah.

Oscar woke as he heard a car door slam, and he barked sharply to wake Hannah and Grandma, who were dozing, too. It felt very late.

"Dad!" Hannah ran into the hallway. "What happened? Is Zach okay? Where is he? Where's Mom?"

Dad looked exhausted. "Grandma

told you he fell off the jungle gym at preschool?"

Hannah nodded. Grandma had broken the news after the play.

"He hit his head. Six stitches, can you believe it? He has to stay at the hospital tonight because it was a head injury, and your mom's staying with him." He sat down wearily on the stairs to take off his shoes. "Hannah, sweetheart, I'm so sorry we missed your play. I was really looking forward to it. We didn't know how seriously Zach had been hurt. Mom got a call saying he'd gone to the hospital in an ambulance."

Hannah sucked in a breath. That made it sound really serious. "Will he be okay?" she asked again, worriedly.

"They think he'll be fine." Dad was

trying to sound reassuring, but he mostly just sounded tired. "Come on. Let's have some hot chocolate and all go to bed."

Grandma stayed the night, and breakfast the next morning was strange with her there but no Mom and Zach. She dropped Hannah off at school, but Dad promised that Mom and Zach would be home from the hospital later that day.

Mom met Hannah at school, but without Zach. She grabbed Hannah in a huge hug.

"Where's Zach? He isn't still in the hospital, is he?" Hannah looked up at Mom anxiously.

Mom shook her head. "It's all right,

sweetie. He's at home with Grandma. He's miserable, but in a couple of days he'll be fine—he'll probably have a scar, though. Hannah, I went to see Mrs. James in the office, and she said we can get a copy of the DVD of the play. I'm just so sorry we weren't there for the real thing. Did it go all right? Did you enjoy it?"

Hannah nodded. It felt mean to say that actually, she hadn't enjoyed the play all that much, because she'd known something must be wrong. "I remembered all my words."

Mom hugged her again, and Hannah was pretty sure that her mom knew what she wasn't saying. "You couldn't help it, Mom. It's okay, honest."

Her mom sighed. "I still can't help

feeling like we let you down."

"I really didn't mind." Hannah nodded firmly. Deep inside, she did wish that they'd been there, of course. But when they got home and she saw Zach lying on the couch, with a huge bandage on his head, she couldn't feel annoyed with him at all. She sat next to Zach all evening, letting him watch the racing car program she couldn't stand, and rubbing Oscar's ears with him.

At least now that the play was over and Christmas vacation had started, Hannah would have a lot more time to spend with Oscar. She wanted to make sure his first Christmas was extra special. She was planning a bunch of long walks, maybe with Nicky, too, and plenty of afternoons curled up on the couch watching all the good movies that were on over vacation. She was even planning to show Oscar *101 Dalmatians* for the first time!

What made it even more thrilling was that it had snowed. The very first morning of vacation, Hannah had woken up to find a light dusting on the street, as though someone had shaken powdered sugar over a cake. It had snowed again that night, just a little more, and the weather forecasters were promising a white Christmas.

Oscar loved it, although he wasn't sure about getting chilly, wet paws. He liked to watch the snow, too, sitting on the back of the couch with his nose pressed up against the window, snapping his teeth at the flakes twirling down outside.

In all the excitement, Hannah had forgotten that her aunt was coming to stay for Christmas. She lived in England, so she and Zach didn't get to see her very often, and this was the first time she'd meet Oscar.

Unfortunately, Aunt Jackie didn't really like dogs. She didn't want Oscar in the living room all the time, and she kept brushing at her clothes, as though Oscar's hair had gotten on them. She was always very dressed up, and she wore a lot of black, so the white hairs really showed up. Hannah took Oscar out in the yard for an extra good grooming session, but it didn't seem to make any difference.

Oscar had never met anyone who didn't like him before. When Aunt Jackie first arrived, he tried to say hello in his normal way, wagging his tail and nuzzling at her legs, and looking up at her with his funny Dalmatian smile. But she stepped back nervously.

"Oh! Why is it showing its teeth like that? Does it bite?" Aunt Jackie looked horrified.

"Of course not!" Hannah cried. "He's just being friendly. And his name is Oscar."

"Put him in the kitchen, Hannah," Mom said quickly. Hannah scowled, but did as she was told. Oscar hadn't done anything wrong! She hoped Aunt Jackie would get used to him.

Oscar was confused. The house was full of strange things, like that big flashy tree that wobbled and jingled. And that strange lady kept pushing him away, and Hannah seemed to be with her all the time. So he stayed on his own in the kitchen on his cushion, feeling miserable.

Hannah did her best to cheer him up, and she did manage to take Oscar for a couple of walks, but Mom kept saying that Aunt Jackie wasn't here for long, and it was rude to go off without her. Hannah thought about suggesting that Aunt Jackie come, too, but she didn't think that would go over very well. She did love Aunt Jackie—she just wished that her aunt liked dogs, too.

Oscar curled up on his cushion, feeling lonely. He tucked his nose under his tail and imagined a long run in the woods, with Hannah laughing and jumping beside him. She'd played with him in the yard that morning, but it just wasn't the same. And now they'd all gone out. Hannah had promised they would be back soon, but they had been gone for a while. Oscar turned around grumpily. He was sick of his cushion, and the kitchen.

Maybe now would be a good time to go and look at that strange tree again. He trotted into the living room and gazed up at it. He didn't trust it, and he wasn't sure why it was in his house.

Sniffing suspiciously, Oscar walked all around the tree, which was surrounded by wrapped packages. The twirly ribbon on one of them caught around his paw, and he shook it. It sprang back. Oscar patted the ribbon with his paw. It was trying to escape!

He seized the package in his teeth, shaking it back and forth fiercely— he loved the feel of the paper tearing. Then he settled down happily to chew the long, pink woolly thing that was inside.

When Hannah, Zach, their parents, and Aunt Jackie walked in from their Christmas shopping trip a little while later, Oscar was fast asleep on the living-room floor. He was surrounded by shreds of silver wrapping paper and twirly ribbon, and the ruins of the pretty, fluffy pink scarf that had been Aunt Jackie's Christmas present for Hannah.

"Oh! Look what that naughty dog has done!" Aunt Jackie cried. "You really need to get him to behave. He's ruined Hannah's present!"

Oscar woke up and slunk guiltily over to Hannah, trailing pink ribbons.

"Bad dog, Oscar!" Mom said angrily.

"You aren't!" Hannah whispered, cuddling him. She looked up at Mom. "It isn't really his fault. We left him alone all day. I know he was naughty, but it's because he's bored!" Then she added very quietly, "And I didn't like that scarf anyway, Oscar...."

Chapter Seven
Company for Christmas

Everyone woke early on Christmas Day. Hannah and Zach were desperate to open their stockings, and Mom and Dad had to start cooking Christmas dinner. Nana was coming, and their other grandma and grandpa, and Uncle Mark and his family—Hannah and Zach's three little cousins. Dad had bought an enormous turkey. Oscar was sitting by the oven looking hopeful—it smelled so good!

Hannah was really looking forward to seeing her cousins again, but she was worried about Oscar. Jamie, Tara, and Phoebe were all young—Phoebe was only two, like Zach—and they weren't really used to dogs. Hannah had a horrible feeling they would be running around trying to hug Oscar all day, and he wasn't going to like it.

Luckily, Oscar loved his Christmas present from her, a really big chewy bone, and that distracted him for a little while, even when Uncle Mark and all the children arrived. But then they spotted Oscar lying on his cushion.

"Hello, doggie!" Phoebe squealed.

"Oooohh!" Tara cried excitedly.

"Can I play with him?" Tara didn't even wait for an answer. She ran straight at Oscar and sat down on his cushion next to him.

Oscar jumped back in horrified surprise. One minute he'd been happily chewing his new bone, and the next minute somebody was trying to grab it from him! He looked up at Hannah pleadingly, begging her to rescue him.

"Tara, Oscar's cushion is his special place," Hannah started to explain. "He doesn't like other people sitting on it."

Tara's face darkened. "Don't boss me around!" she told Hannah angrily.

"I'm not," Hannah sighed. She gave Oscar a gentle pat, and he clambered off his cushion and scuttled out into the hallway.

Everywhere Oscar went that morning, Aunt Jackie kept glancing nervously at him, or one of the cousins was grabbing at him. And then Uncle Mark accidentally kicked him when he was sitting under the table hoping for a treat during Christmas dinner. Oscar dashed out from under the table with a howl, and Hannah scooped him up and cuddled him.

"You're having a bad day, aren't you, Oscar?" she said. "Poor sweetie. Mom, can I give Oscar a little bit of turkey? Please? Just to cheer him up?"

Mom looked doubtful, but then she said, "Oh, I suppose as a Christmas treat. But in his food bowl in the kitchen, Hannah, so he doesn't think he's being fed from the table."

Hannah nodded and tried not to look guilty. She quite often slipped Oscar pieces of food under the table. She knew she shouldn't, but he had such good eyes for begging with.

The turkey was the best part of the day for Oscar. It was delicious, and he forgot about the noisy, grabby children while he was wolfing it down. But as soon as Christmas dinner was finished, he saw Jamie slipping down from his chair and reaching out to pet him. Oscar made a dash for it out of the living room, where Mom and Dad had set up a folding table for dinner.

Out in the hallway he headed for his hiding place under the stairs, wriggling right to the back under a pile of coats.

"Where did your dog go?" Jamie asked Hannah.

Hannah crossed her fingers behind her back. "I don't know," she told him. She didn't, actually; it wasn't a total lie. But she very much suspected he was hiding under the stairs.

Dad called Jamie to come back into the living room, telling everyone that a really good movie was about to start, and the little boy ran off. Hannah gave a relieved sigh. If she helped Mom finish clearing the table and everyone else was watching the movie, maybe she could sneak off and give Oscar a cuddle on his own—without any cousins or little brothers wanting to join in.

Oscar lay there in the dark, remembering the taste of the turkey, and wishing Hannah was there. But he didn't dare come out of his hiding place to find her.

Hannah carried the last of the empty dessert bowls into the kitchen and piled them up next to all the other plates. "I'm just going to check on Oscar," she told her mom.

"Oh, yes," Mom said. "He's not really enjoying all these people, is he? Do you want to stay in here with him for a little while? I don't think he'll want to go in the living room."

"Won't Aunt Jackie and Nana and Grandma and everyone think I'm being rude?" Hannah asked.

Mom laughed. "I think they're all going to fall asleep watching this movie, Hannah; everyone's so full of food. It'll be fine."

"Thanks, Mom." Hannah hugged her.

Her mom hugged her back, but then let go quickly. "Oh, no! What's Zach screaming about?" And she hurried off to the living room to sort it out.

Hannah sighed. Zach again, just when she'd been having a nice moment with Mom. She padded out into the hallway, spotting Mom cuddling a still-wailing Zach. Jamie and Tara were moaning that they couldn't hear the movie, and Phoebe looked like she might join in the howling.

Hannah squeezed herself into the alcove under the stairs and giggled as a chilly little nose dabbed at her hand. "You've got the right idea, Oscar," she told him. "It's a nightmare out there!"

Oscar nuzzled her gratefully, feeling sure that she would protect him from the other children. He climbed into her lap and huffed out a satisfied little yawn. He was safe now that Hannah was with him.

Hannah petted him thoughtfully. "It's a little squished for me under here, Oscar." She sighed. "But I really don't want to go and watch that movie with all the others." She could still hear Zach moaning, and Mom was sounding as though she was losing patience. Then Hannah brightened, a smile curving her lips. "Let's go for a walk, Oscar! A special Christmas walk."

Oscar scrambled down from her lap, his tail wagging. He knew what walk meant, and he definitely approved of the idea.

"Let's go and ask Mom." Hannah hauled herself out of the gap under the stairs.

But when she peeked around the living-room door, with Oscar peeking around her legs, Zach's moans had progressed into a full-blown temper tantrum. Mom and Dad strode past— Dad carrying Zach, and Mom looking embarrassed and angry. It wasn't the time to go asking about walks.

But Oscar was looking up at her so hopefully. Hannah frowned. "I know. We'll leave a note for Mom on the kitchen table. I'm sure it'll be okay."

She grabbed Oscar's leash and wrapped herself in her warmest things, putting on an extra pair of socks before stepping into her boots. The snow was thick outside.

The living-room door was partly open, and she could see that Grandma was asleep on the couch, with little Phoebe asleep on her. Hannah didn't want to wake them, or disturb the others watching the movie. She wrote a quick note, promising to be back soon, and left it on the kitchen table. With a sudden excited smile, she took a couple of carrots from the vegetable drawer. Then she and Oscar slipped quietly out the front door.

A few minutes later, Mom came down after settling Zach to sleep. She took the mince pies out of the living room, just in case Oscar tried to nibble them, and put down the plate on the kitchen table—right on top of Hannah's note.

Chapter Eight
A Special Walk

Oscar padded happily through the crisp snow, his paws crunching at every step. It felt good, and he wanted to run. He looked up hopefully at Hannah. She laughed, and they raced down the road.

"I've got some carrots," Hannah told Oscar when they stopped, panting, the cold air burning their throats. "Should we go and see the horses?"

They walked past Hannah's school, where the playground was a sheet of snow, without a single footprint. At last, they reached the riding school fields. The horses were standing clustered together, looking rather mournful.

"The carrots will cheer them up," Hannah told Oscar. As they reached the fence, she boosted Oscar up so that he had his paws on the top slat, and she rested his bottom against her. "Ooh, Oscar, I'm not sure how long I can do this," she told him. "You're definitely getting heavier!"

She held the carrots out invitingly, and the horses came trotting over.

Oscar wagged his tail delightedly and stretched out his nose to nuzzle at the horses as they gobbled the carrots.

"Be careful they don't accidentally nibble you, too," Hannah warned him, laughing as she pulled him away. They watched happily as the horses nosed around, looking for more carrots. Finally, they gave up and wandered off.

Hannah sighed. "I guess we should go home. It's starting to snow again. Look!"

Oscar gazed up at her. He could tell from her tone that she didn't really want to, and he wagged his tail hopefully.

"I guess we could stay out a little longer," Hannah said slowly. "It isn't getting dark yet, and I don't think anyone will have missed us." She sighed again and hugged Oscar close, feeling suddenly lonely.

But her sad mood was quickly broken as Oscar licked her face lavishly, making her splutter and giggle. "Okay. Let's go to the woods, huh? We can walk down to the stream. It might even be frozen!"

They tramped along the snowy path, Hannah admiring the layer of crystal snow decorating the branches as they drew closer to the woods. It had drifted deeply under the trees, and Hannah and Oscar ran along, kicking up the snow, Oscar barking happily. His barks echoed around the empty forest, and Hannah chased him in and out of the dark trees.

Oscar felt better than he had in a long time. All the grumpiness was gone. He shook his ears and barked, then barked again as a pile of snow fell down from a branch with a shivery thump.

At last, they settled down to rest on a fallen tree by the edge of the stream. It was so beautiful—the stream was just starting to ice over at the edges. Hannah sighed happily. This was much better than sitting in the stuffy house. But they should probably go back soon, or it would be getting dark. She looked up at the sky and realized with a start that the sun was out again, but it was low in the sky, and the shadows had grown longer and darker. They must have been out longer than she had thought. She sprang up anxiously. "We need to go home, Oscar. It's late."

Oscar looked up at her and wagged his tail uncertainly. Hannah sounded upset.

She looked around, her eyes wide. "Oscar, which way did we come? I can only see our footsteps right here by the fallen tree. The snow has covered the rest of them." She shook herself angrily. "Oh, this is silly. We can't be lost." She walked around the tree trunk, looking carefully at the little paths leading off between the trees. Which one had they come along? Panic was growing inside her, and her heart was racing. Every time she looked up, the sky was a deeper shade of eerie nighttime blue.

"It's this one, I think," she muttered uncertainly. "Come on, Oscar." She didn't notice Oscar looking back as they set off down the path. He sniffed at the tree trunks thoughtfully as they walked. Why were they going this way?

"This isn't right," Hannah said anxiously after a few minutes. "We should be coming out of the trees by now. We'll have to go back." She led Oscar down the path again, stumbling over the snow in the gathering dark. Back at the clearing by the stream, Hannah sat down again, for her legs were shaking. She had to admit that she didn't know the way.

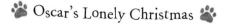

They were lost.

Oscar looked up at Hannah, confused. She was crying, and he didn't know why. He leaned his head against her leg lovingly, and she looked down and patted him.

"I'm scared, Oscar," she told him. "And it's so cold. I just want to go home."

Oscar bounced up, wagging his tail. He knew home, and he could get there. Was that all Hannah wanted? He pulled gently on his leash and gave a little whine. When she looked up, he barked, telling her to follow.

Hannah blinked. "Home?" she asked. "Can you get us home, Oscar?"

Oscar tugged his leash, and Hannah stumbled after him. The path he chose looked just like all the others to her, but he seemed so sure. Every so often he would stop to sniff at the bushes, then he'd wag his tail and pull her on.

Hannah looked around doubtfully, but Oscar knew exactly where he was going. He trotted on through the woods, and at last she saw the riding school fields at the end of the path.

"Oh, Oscar, you're amazing!" she said, crouching down to give him a hug. "But we have to hurry up and get home." Then her shoulders drooped. "Actually, I suppose it doesn't matter, except that I'm getting really cold, and I bet you are, too. I shouldn't think anyone will have noticed we've been gone."

They trudged home, past the school, and turned at last onto their street. Oscar pricked up his ears as they came around the corner, and Hannah stopped in surprise. Someone was calling her name. And there it was again. It sounded like Grandma.

"Hannah! Hannah!" And that was her dad.

Hannah started walking again, Oscar pulling her down the road. Nana, and Grandma and Grandpa, Dad, and Uncle Mark, and even Aunt Jackie were out in her street, all calling for her.

They *had* missed her, then! Her dad looked really worried, and Hannah slowed down a little, realizing that he was probably going to be furious.

"Hannah!" Dad caught sight of her and ran up the street, swinging her into his arms and squeezing her tightly. "Where were you? We were so worried. We had no idea where you were!"

"I left a note!" Hannah said, surprised.

"You and Mom were busy with Zach, and Oscar was so miserable.... I'm sorry," she added. "I didn't mean to be so late. I got lost in the woods, and Oscar found the way home. He's really smart."

Dad was still holding her as though he thought she might disappear. "We didn't find a note. Oh, Hannah, you should have told us."

"But Zach was screaming…."

"It's okay—we're not angry. We were scared, Hannah. Please promise you'll never go off like that again."

"I won't. Promise." Hannah nodded.

Dad crouched down to pet Oscar. "He brought Hannah home," he told everyone as they came up the path. "Get inside, Hannah; you must be frozen."

"Oscar brought you back?" Aunt Jackie asked in surprise. "But he's still just a puppy! Clever boy, Oscar!" And she reached down and patted him gently.

Hannah beamed—Aunt Jackie had never petted Oscar before.

"Hannah!" Zach came running to hug her, and then he hugged Oscar, too.

"We were so worried about you!" Mom told her.

"I'm sorry," Hannah whispered, but she was watching Zach and Oscar worriedly. Then she realized that Oscar didn't have his ears laid back, and he was thumping his tail on the hall floor.

"Wow!" Mom said. "Oscar's not being nervous around Zach." She looked at Oscar thoughtfully. "I guess he's just had a really good, long walk. You've exercised some of his nerves away, Hannah." Then she frowned as Zach tried to pick Oscar up. "No, Zach. You can pet Oscar, but you don't pull him around, okay?"

Hannah looked at Mom in amazement as she gently pulled Zach away. "Come on. Oscar's tired, and he wants to go and lie on his cushion now. You play with your new airplane. Grandma and Grandpa want to see it." Zach made a face, but he did as he was told, and Mom looked over at Hannah. "What is it?"

"You *never* make Zach leave Oscar alone!" Hannah gasped.

Mom sighed. "Well, we probably should have. Oscar's a patient dog, but Zach needs to be a bit more gentle. We've been letting him get away with stuff because he's little, but this is important. I'm sorry, Hannah. I know it's hard being the big sister sometimes."

"Thanks, Mom!" Hannah threw her arms around her. Then she let go, looking thoughtfully through the living-room door at Zach playing with their grandparents. "Oscar is Zach's dog, too, though. I probably should let him join in more." She sighed, and then brightened up. "When we start dog training, do you think Zach can come, too? He might learn to be more gentle with Oscar if he saw everybody at dog training being really careful with their dogs."

"That's a great idea," Mom replied. "We need to get going and book those classes after Christmas. But right now, Oscar deserves a bit more turkey, don't you think? Come on, Oscar!"

Hannah nodded, then she put her head around the living-room door. "Zach! Do you want to come and give Oscar some turkey?"

Zach jumped up and took Hannah's hand. They followed Oscar as he trotted eagerly into the kitchen, and watched him gobble up the turkey. He pushed the bowl around the floor, licking around the sides, making sure he hadn't missed any. Then he sighed happily, licked Hannah's foot, and slumped down on his cushion.

Hannah giggled, and Zach giggled, too, looking up at his big sister. Oscar was stretched out on his cushion with his nose in one corner and his back paws almost touching the other. He thumped his tail just a little as he heard them laugh. Then he sighed and wriggled himself back into a ball—worn out, and full, and very, very happy to be home.